A

TRAIN

JOURNEY

A JOURNEY THAT TURNS

PARANORMAL

PANTHPREET SINGH

DEDICATION

This book is dedicated to my mom for believing in me and encouraging me to follow my dreams.

A TRAIN JOURNEY

<u>CHARACTER SKETCH</u>:-"Avinash" is the person who does not believe in ghosts at all. "Alia" is the one who is worried about ghosts. "Sparsh" is the clever one who neither believes nor ignores them. He cares about the friendship and does not let "Avinash" and "Alia" argue about their beliefs.

<u>BACKGROUND</u>:- There are three best friends named Avinash, Sparsh, and Alia. Avinash and Sparsh are male, while Alia is female. They have been together in the same school since kindergarten. During their farewell, they sit separately and feel emotional. They promise each other that once they complete their undergraduate programs, they will reunite for a night train journey to Kerala. Avinash goes abroad for his studies, Sparsh goes to an IIT, and Alia gets admission to AIIMS. The day comes when they finally board the train. However, as soon as Alia gets on the train, the gates get locked, and the train starts moving. Alia notices a man who is trying to get on the train but misses it. Later, the camera shows that the man was asking them not to board the train.

"The train came to a stop, and the lights flickered on and off, causing Alia to feel frightened. Avinash reacted by punching the train and exclaiming, "What the heck?" The train then resumed its journey. Sparsh noticed that there was an LED screen on the train displaying "LEVEL 1."

LEVEL ONE:-

As the train came to a stop, the LED display flashed a message: "Bring me the novel." Avinash, Sparsh, and Alia quickly disembarked and found themselves standing in front of a hospital. They could hear faint noises emanating from inside, so they decided to investigate.

Inside the hospital, the three of them split up to cover more ground. Alia walked down a corridor and saw a nurse in a professional dress standing at the end of the hallway. She ran towards the nurse, but as she got closer, the nurse vanished into thin air. Suddenly, she heard screams coming from another part of the hospital and became frightened.

As she turned to flee, a cold hand touched her shoulder. Alia spun around and came face-to-face with the nurse, whose eyes were now red and lips stained with blood. Terrified, Alia let out a piercing scream that alerted Avinash and Sparsh, who came running to her aid.

Alia recounted her encounter with the nurse, but Avinash didn't believe her. Sparsh, however, believed that they were in some sort of game and that the nurse was a clue. They decided to stick together and search for the novel as a team.

Together, they explored the hospital, looking for clues and trying to make sense of what was happening. They found themselves in a maze of corridors, some of which led to dark, ominous rooms. As they walked, they couldn't shake off the feeling that they were being watched. Their hearts raced as they tried to stay calm and focused on their mission.

As they progressed, they started to piece together the clues. They realized that they were in a game where they had to solve puzzles and complete levels to survive. They were determined to make it to the end and find their way out of the game.

<u>THE SEARCH</u>: Sparsh asks Avinash and Alia to stop, and suddenly he has a brilliant idea. "The Library! Yes, a Library! That's where we could find that Novel," he exclaimed with a glint in his eye. Avinash and Alia were impressed by his suggestion, and the three of them began their search for the Library.

As they were moving around the hospital, Avinash suddenly shouted, "Guys, check this out!" He had found the blueprint of the hospital. The three of them studied the blueprint and located the Library. They started making their way towards it, but then Alia realized that they were getting lost. They were coming back to the same spot again and again.

Suddenly, Alia remembered seeing the word "Librarian" on a nurse's uniform. "Wait, I think I've got it," she said. "Let's move to the room where I saw the nurse with the word 'Librarian' on her uniform." They quickly made their way to the room and found that it was the Library itself.

In the Library, A found a radio, but the sound was not very clear. When Avinash and Sparsh moved closer to the radio, they heard a chilling voice say, "Welcome To The Library." The three of them were terrified and started running. They then locked themselves in an empty room where the objects looked as though they had not been used in over a decade. The room was filled with a musty smell, and the objects were covered in a thick layer of dust. The silence was deafening.

As Avinash looks around the room, their eyes fall on a photo that catches their attention. The picture shows a group of kids standing with a nurse who looks content and happy. The children in the photo also seem to be overjoyed, with smiles on their faces. Avinash can't help but wonder about the story behind the photo and the people in it.

Suddenly, Sparsh's memory is jogged by the image. He remembers that once his grandpa read him a news about a nurse who lived in a hospital with abandoned children. The nurse was a kind and compassionate person who took care of the children as if they were her own. Despite facing financial difficulties, she ensured that the children had a roof over their heads, food in their bellies, and were educated.

In the story, the nurse approached some politicians for help, hoping that they would assist her in ensuring her children's education and a better future.

The politician promised her that he would soon visit the hospital with the help. Later that day nurse heard a jeep coming and was so happy that the politician came to help but the truth was something else. The politician came with other men and physically abused her and burnt the hospital with the kids inside.

The novel was based on this incident, written by one of the children the woman had adopted in the past. However, the politician had murdered the writer and buried him together with the manuscript in the hospital's parking lot. When they rushed to the parking area, Sparsh was the one who discovered the body, as it had not been properly buried. As soon as he took the novel the 3 heard a whistle, it was the same train. The 3 quickly get onto the train and the train starts moving.

Alia was crying so hard and was so scared and suddenly Avinash asked them to look at the LED Screen which displayed "LEVEL 2".

LEVEL:- 2

The LED display reads "Bring me the Report". Alia becomes emotional and starts crying, saying "We are stuck in this game forever, we won't make it". Sparsh stands up, wipes Alia's tears, and declares with a spark in his eyes, "We will make it out for sure, and demand justice for the nurse and those innocent kids". Avinash shouts, "Have you gone mad? You still care about that bloody nurse who almost killed us!" Sparsh responds, "The nurse never harmed us, or she might have been trying to help us...". Before Sparsh could finish his sentence, the train stopped, and the gates opened. This time, the three of them get out of the train with confidence and spark, but without fear. The novel glows as they exit the train, but no one notices. They find themselves in a town with no one but only an empty school and a spine-chilling forest nearby. Confused and searching for a clue, Sparsh suddenly halts Avinash and Alia, saying, "If this is a game, the levels must give some hints for the upcoming level. What if we already have a clue, but we're not noticing it?". Avinash has a sudden realization, saying "The novel! Yes, the novel must be the clue". Avinash asks Alia to open the novel, but Alia expresses confusion, saying it's about the story of that nurse, and questioning the relation. Sparsh interrupts and confirms that Avinash is right, and they should open the novel. As they open the novel, they realize that an extra chapter has been added, titled "THE REPORT".

THE REPORT:- They sat in a triangle at a house and began reading the chapter carefully to learn more about the report. The chapter tells the story of a young boy named Oliver who was relentlessly bullied and abused by his older classmates. One day, while out walking his dog Charlie in the park, he noticed that the bullies were also there. Trying to avoid them, he took a different path, but unfortunately, one of the bullies noticed him and threw a stone at him to get his attention. Charlie barks alert, Oliver forgets the collar, and Charlie runs to bite a bully. The next morning, Oliver asked his single-parent father if he could stay home from school as he was feeling sick. However, his father joyfully insisted him to attend school. When Oliver arrived at school, he saw that the bullies were waiting for him outside his classroom. In an attempt to avoid them, he ran towards the washroom. Unfortunately, the bullies spotted him and locked him inside the school's storeroom for the entire day. When the school got off they visited the storeroom and took their belts and wooden sticks and started beating the kid, he shouted for help but there was no one in the school, they beat him so hard that the kid lost his life. The bullies got scared as they knew his father was a policeman. The bullies then buried his body in the forest nearby and left the forest.

That evening, Oliver's father went to visit his son's class
teacher to inquire about his whereabouts. However, the
teacher informed him that Oliver did not attend school
that day. Oliver's father, with tears in his eyes and a low
voice, asked her if she was sure because he had left for
school in the morning but had not returned yet. Later
that evening, Charlie, Oliver's dog, went out for his walk
and followed his nose to the forest where he discovered
Oliver's body. There was one of the bullies feeling sorry
for what he did to the kid and tearfully patted the dog
but someone from nowhere shot Charlie. This was
another bully with a gun in his hand and asked the boy
to calm down and not to cry like a woman. He leaves
the place but the other buries Charlie beside Oliver's
body and leaves the forest with a heavy heart and teary
eyes as he feels sorry for Oliver and his Dog. He went to

visit Oliver's father and told him the whole truth. In response, the policeman slapped him tightly and promised, "All of you will soon be behind bars". He filed a First Information Report (FIR) at his local police station, but weeks passed without any action taken, as the bullies were the sons of powerful individuals in the state. He tore the FIR report out of the file, and with it in hand, he committed suicide. He was so devastated that he could not even bring himself to discover his son's body. Oliver and Charlie were his only family, and he could not bear the pain of injustice.

As Sparsh finished telling the story, the three of them heard a voice saying "You will be behind bars soon". They followed the voice and it led them to a room where they saw a man holding a report and crying. He apologized and said, "I'm sorry, son. I couldn't get justice for you and Charlie."

Out of nowhere, the man vanished, only to reappear right in front of the three individuals. He shouted, "My son has the report!" The three were left stunned and confused, wondering how they could retrieve the report from his son, who was already dead. Suddenly, Sparsh whispered in a worried voice, "The body might have the report." As they passed the school on their way to the forest, they heard a child's laughter. Although they had no idea where the bodies were buried, they felt that certain steps were leading them to a particular spot. They decided to follow the steps and stumbled upon the body. They retrieved the report and shouted, "Oliver and Charlie will be served justice!".

As usual, the trio boards the train but while boarding C notices a pair of eyes following them, disappearing into the forest.

Sparsh says, "That's so strange". Avinash and Alia asked what happened. A asked them to look at the LED. The LED still displayed LEVEL 2.

Alia was already tense about something else, not the screen. Avinash and Sparsh asked what happened. Alia told them about the eyes she saw in the forest, and Avinash confessed that he saw some sort of eyes in the hospital too. Sparsh headed down and said a soliloquy, "Why not me?" As he saw, he jumped off the seat out of fear and shouted, "Oliver!" The train then stopped, and they immediately ran out of the train.

Alia stopped and said, "This is not the complete report. A part of the report is still missing." "My son has the report," said Avinash. Sparsh shouted, "Charlie! Mr. Michael used to call Charlie his son as well."

They ran to Charlie's grave and unburied his body. When they took a close look at Charlie, he opened his eyes, and Avinash and Alia ran out of fear. Sparsh did not run; he tearfully patted Charlie and asked for the report. Charlie smiled and vanished into the sand, and Sparsh found another part of the report. However, he was shocked because the report contained the names of the bullies, and to his surprise, Avinash's, Sparsh's, and Alia's names were also mentioned. Sparsh's name was typewritten along with the others, but Avinash's and Alia's names were written in blood.

Avinash and Alia were visibly worried when they approached Sparsh. Sparhs asked them what was wrong, and Avinash explained that the school they were standing in front of was the same one they had all attended. This jogged Alia's memory of an incident that happened years before when she and Avinash stayed behind after school to have a secret party in the auditorium. While they were sneaking snacks to the auditorium, Alia heard someone shout "Help me, please." She dismissed it as a mistake but then heard the same cry again. She told Avinash about it, but he thought she was joking and laughed it off. They

continued on to the auditorium, but Alia couldn't shake the feeling that something was wrong. However, Avinash was not convinced why Sparsh's name appeared on the report.

Alia stated, "It all makes sense now, we are all somehow connected to the incidents mentioned in this novel". However, Avinash disagreed, as it wasn't just about that one incident but also the hospital... before Avinash could finish his statement, Alia's eyes started turning red, and her body began to vanish. Avinash and Sparsh became extremely worried and started shouting, "What's happening? What should we do?" Alia interrupted them, saying, "Not we, I am related to the incident." She then appeared in her nurse avatar and revealed that she herself was the nurse who was abused and burnt alive in the hospital, along with the children. She glared at Sparsh with mixed emotions, but with anger, and then disappeared. Avinash and Sparsh were heartbroken and got onto the train but without Alia this time. Avinash slapped Sparsh and punched him in the face. Sparsh angrily asked, "What are you doing? Why did you punch me?" Avinash demanded to know how Sparsh knew the policeman's name, which had not been mentioned anywhere. Sparsh was forced to tell the truth before they could leave the train.

THE TRUTH:-Sparsh confided in Avinash that he and their classmates used to bully Oliver because he was American and not Indian. Sparsh admitted that he was the one who went to Oliver's house and told Mr. Michael the truth. Avinash was distraught and asked Sparsh why he would do something so cruel to a kid. Sparsh emotionally explained that he used to make fun of Oliver, but he never bullied him like the others did.

Suddenly, the lights on the train went out, and it started shaking as if there was an earthquake. The bright LED display made it difficult to read the message. After a moment, the train stabilized, and the lights came back on. The LED display showed a clear message: "THE FINAL LEVEL"

THE FINAL LEVEL:-

As Avinash and Sparsh exited the train, they suddenly stood in a cemetery. Without warning, a gust of wind blew a report directly into Sparsh's face. As he removed the report, he was shocked to see Mr. Michael standing before him. Before Sparsh could even react, Mr. Michael reached out and removed his heart from his chest with his bare hands before disappearing into thin air.

Avinash was so frightened that he ran away from where he was. On his way to a safe shelter, he saw Alia and hugged her tightly, however, he quickly realized that the one he hugged was not her but someone else. He immediately ran away from there and found a safe shelter. Later, he heard Alia's voice calling out to him to come out. But Avinash was not sure if it was Alia or someone else imitating her. He waited cautiously until he was sure it was her, and then he sneaked out to meet her.

He went to her and tearfully said, "I am so sorry for what happened to you ". She wiped off his tears and told him for him to pass this level he would have to cremate the bodies of the kids who were brutally burnt

alive in the hospital. The bodies were inside the wooden boxes in the cemetery right in front of Avinash. For this, he planned to fire the whole place but had no idea how he would do that. Suddenly Alia disappears in the cold wind but this time without the Novel. Avinash opened the Novel and noticed an extra chapter was added to the Novel titled 'The Cremation'

THE CREMATION: As soon as he opens the chapter, the texts disappear. Now the Novel was just a blank book but nothing more. He then heard a sound as someone was trying to come out of the wooden box, he fearfully unlocked the box and found Oliver standing in front of him. He tearfully in a deep voice apologizes to Oliver on behalf of his friend Sparsh. Oliver smiles, points toward the Novel, and disappears. As Avinash opened the novel, he noticed an arrow pointing to the right.

Following the arrow, he saw an old building in the distance.

As he entered the building, he had a feeling that someone was following him. The sound of footsteps grew louder and closer, prompting him to run. He turned around, but nothing was there. As he faced forward, a crying girl appeared before him. Surprisingly she was alive, she told Avinash that she lost all of her friends and was the only one to survive so far. She apologized for not heeding his warning to avoid boarding the train. Before she could finish her sentence, someone dragged her into the darkness, and she vanished. Although Avinash was concerned about the bodies, he couldn't help but wonder why the girl had said he warned them not to board the train.

He then noticed a gate. As he opened it, he could see some stairs leading downwards. However, it was too dark to see what was down there. Despite the darkness, he was brave enough to decide to explore and see if there was anything helpful downstairs. As he descended, the visibility improved, and he noticed a fuel tank beside him. He felt happy and immediately picked up the fuel tank. However, as he began to climb back up the stairs, the gate suddenly closed, and he fell due to fear.

He panicked but remembered he had a lighter that
Sparsh gave him before boarding the train. He took a
stick, poured the fuel over it, and fired it up. He then
saw a tunnel, he went inside along with a fuel tank and
the "Mashal" he made. There were loud sounds of a
bunch of kids crying and asking for help. Avinash walked
wearily with tears streaming down his face and finally
spotted the cemetery at the end of the tunnel. He
hurried towards the boxes, poured the fuel, and lit
them up. However, it started raining just as he set them
alight. To his surprise, the fire did not go out. In the dark
sky, he saw the shadows of his friends, including a man,
some kids, and a dog. Upon closer inspection, he
recognized them as Mr. Michael, Oliver, and Charlie,
along with the children. As usual, he boarded the train,
the doors closed, and he sat on the floor, crying loudly
as he had lost his friends. This time the train stopped at
a station where there were people and he exited the
train weak and tired. It was a bright day and Avinash
was finally back to his normal life. He saw light after a
very long and hard time and exited the station. As he
left the station, the camera went back to the station
and showed the same guy who tried to stop them at the
very beginning from boarding the train, as the camera
showed the man's face, it was so shocking as it was
Avinash himself. The camera then showed the train's
LED display that displayed "LEVEL 4".

"THE JOURNEY WILL CONTINUE ONCE
MORE..."

ACKNOWLEDGEMENTS______

To God, for your loving guidance and for the many blessings you have bestowed upon me.

To my mother, Mrs. Harvinder Kaur, for your love and support, and for the code of ethics you taught me, which has served me so well in my life.

To my sisters, Jaspreet Kaur and Namanpreet Kaur, for your enthusiastic support of my work.

To my pet Peeco, for always loving me, no matter what.